Max and the Balloons

by Anne Giulieri
illustrated by Martin Bailey

Kate looked and looked.

"Where are my balloons?"
said Kate.

"Are they with you, Mum?"

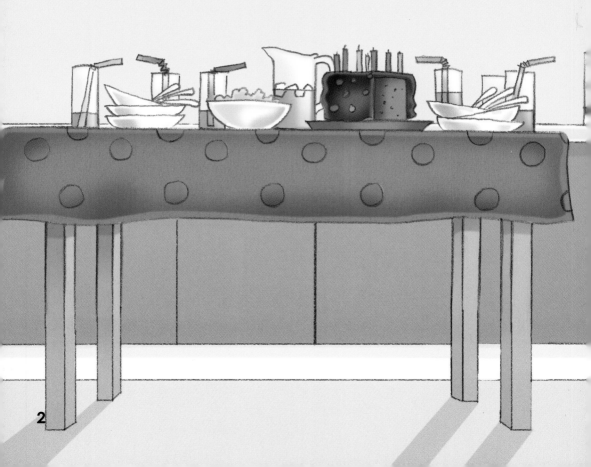

"No," said Mum.

"They are not with me."

"Are the balloons
on your bed?" said Mum.

"Oh, no!" said Kate.
"The balloons
are not on my bed.
Max is on my bed!"

"Max!" said Kate.
"Get off my bed.
Go to your bed!"

Max got off Kate's bed.
He ran to Mum's bed.

"Max!" said Mum.
"Get off my bed!"

"You are
a naughty little dog,"
said Kate.
"You sat on my bed,
and you sat on Mum's bed.
Go to your bed!"

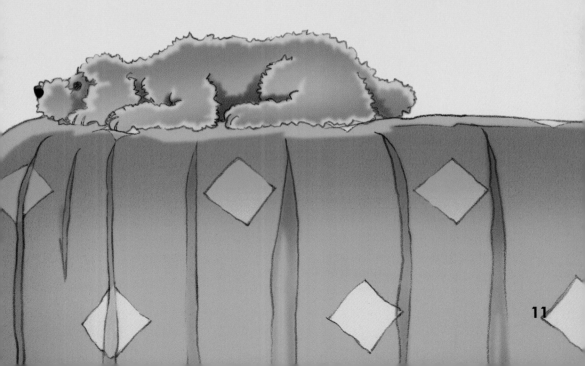

Max went to his bed.

"Oh, Max!" said Kate.
"My balloons
are in **your** bed!"

"Here are your balloons,"
said Mum.

"Oh, Max!" said Kate.
"You are
a **naughty** little dog!"